Never Stop Dreaming

Inspiring short stories of unique and wonderful boys, about courage, self-confidence, talents, and the potential found in all our dreams

Ellen Mills

Special Art Stories

Never Stop Dreaming

Inspiring short stories of unique and wonderful boys, about courage, self-confidence, talents, and the potential found in all our dreams.

Ellen Mills

PAPERBACK ISBN: 979-12-80592-35-4

support@specialartbooks.com
www.specialartbooks.com

Table of Contents

Introduction

"Never give up on what you really want to do. The person with big dreams is more powerful than one with all the facts."

—*Albert Einstein*

Hello, little dreamer,

What's the most incredible dream you've ever had?

Was it about becoming a superhero, who could save the world from danger? Maybe you've dreamed about being a wizard who could create anything he wanted with his spells? It is wonderful to have such magical dreams while you sleep!

But what kind of dreams do you have when you're awake? Do you dream about doing well at school? Or maybe you've dreamed about finding a best friend? What about dreaming of being able to stand on a stage in front of a crowd of people without feeling any fear at all? Not everyone's dreams are the same, but one thing is certain: we *all* have dreams!

Within this book you will find stories of boys who had dreams of their own. Some of them lived in a world that you might recognize, and some of them live in enchanted worlds you've never seen before! But you will be able to see how all of these boys, despite finding difficulties along the way, made their dreams come true.

Like the boys you will read about, you too can discover how no dream is too big to be realized. If you believe in yourself and all the talents and abilities that make you unique, you will have every opportunity to achieve your goals. Don't limit yourself, little dreamer, because a special and wonderful boy like you has all the things you need to make your dreams come true.

Now, let's start this journey of ours, traveling off to places where pirates, astronauts, and wizards face their greatest challenges! And if you look closely enough you might see that even in the most magical of worlds, these boy's dreams might just look a little something like yours.

A Friend from Another World

Have you ever wanted to travel to space and the stars? Maybe you want to visit every planet in the universe and place your flag for all to see! But there may be some dangers ahead that you don't know about. Or maybe some are friendly, but they seem...different. Maybe they spoke a different language, or maybe they didn't look like you. Daniel met some-one, or technically some*thing* like this. But even though it looked different, Daniel wanted to be its friend.

Daniel is an astronaut who loved to travel around the planets. His dream was to put a flag on every planet he landed on so that history would know of his travels! When he gets to one planet, he floats around outside and puts a flag deep into the ground so that it doesn't float away. Why was this his dream? you may ask. Well, it's because whenever Daniel visited a new planet, there was always something exciting to be found. He loved seeing the different wildlife and was amazed at the different things he could find, such as strange looking animals and different types of rocks. Some planets even had more than one moon!

It was discoveries like this that made Daniel love to travel. Because he could see what many other humans never would.

One day, as he put his flag down and went to get back in his rocket, he heard a noise from behind him. When he turned around, a little green alien with three eyes peeked out at him from behind the flag.

Daniel was startled for a moment and waited for the alien to move, but it only stared at him.

"Um...hi." Daniel waved. The alien freaked him out a little. He heard that aliens could be scary and dangerous, especially to humans. They could sneak up and eat people! Or they could possibly spit acid! Either way, Daniel tried to avoid them as much as possible.

The little green alien bounced up and down, before it took his flag and scuttled away.

"Hey!" Daniel called out to the alien. He chased after the alien far from the rocket. "Come back."

After running after the alien for some time he finally caught up to it.

"Excuse me, but I would like... my flag back." Daniel said, a little out of breath from all the chasing.

The alien made a little noise and put the flag on the ground in front of him. Daniel was very hesitant to grab it.

It seemed harmless. But it was something he had never seen before. What if it was part of some mind control species? Maybe it was waiting for him to reach for the flag so it could bite him!

Nevertheless, Daniel had to get his flag back so he could mark the planet. He quickly took the flag back and went back in the direction of his rocket. But when he tried to go towards it, he couldn't remember which way he had run.

"Oh no," he said. "There's got to be a way to get back!" He needed to get back soon. He remembered his parents telling him stories of the creatures that would come out when nightfall came, and he definitely didn't want to find out what they looked like.

Daniel tried to retrace his steps, but unfortunately he still couldn't find his way.

As nightfall came, he found a cave to hide from any of the frightening creatures. He had a snack in his pocket that could keep him full and a little ball that he sat in front of him. He poked the top of the ball and it created a fire to keep him warm. He was worried that his fire would attract other things because his fire was the only light on the planet for miles.

As he sat by the warmth of the flames he heard a little growl not too far from him.

He waited quietly as the growling began to get closer and closer. Daniel kept his eyes closed and waited as the monster was about to eat him!

But then he heard a familiar small sound and saw the green alien come into the cave, excited to see him.

"Oh, it's you," said Daniel. At first he was nervous that the alien would now eat him, as he was cornered. But when the alien bounced up and down in excitement, he began to relax and even smiled. "Honestly, I'm really relieved to see you. I thought there was actually a big creature nearby."

Suddenly, the ground shook as he heard a large roar this time! A shadow fell over the cave and a large hand reached in. Daniel shrank back and tried to stay out of its reach. The little alien scuttled over to the hand and Daniel tried to reach for it.

"Don't! He'll eat you!" Daniel whispered. The little alien opened its mouth and let out a terrifying roar! It was so loud that Daniel had to put his hands over his ears. Hearing this roar, the monster ran away in fear, leaving them alone. The little alien came back to Daniel and bounced happily.

"Wow, uh...thank you." He smiled, took out a snack and then offered it to the alien who happily munched on it.

"Huh, maybe you're not so freaky after all," Daniel laughed. He began to make conversation with the alien and told them about his travels. The alien listened carefully and jumped up and down in excitement whenever he mentioned running from crazy events. He then yawned as the night went on and began to fall asleep. The alien watched over him the whole night until morning. When Daniel woke up, the alien was gone and Daniel was sad that he had left. He came out of the cave and saw green footprints leading off into the distance. Daniel followed the footprints for a few minutes until they stopped at his rocket.

"I can't believe it! My rocket!" Daniel cheered. He was happy he had found it again. But where was the alien? He couldn't leave without thanking them for their help. Daniel looked around his rocket and to see if they were maybe hiding under it. He then tried to call out for them.

"Green alien! Green alien! Where are you?" he called out. He listened carefully, but he heard nothing.

Giving up, he climbed into his rocket and buckled in. He looked out the window one more time to see if there was any sign of them. Nothing.

He boosted up his rocket and began to lift off into space. As he floated in the stars, he heard the faint sound of something familiar. He put the rocket on autopilot and walked through the rocket. The farther he walked through, the louder the noise got. He reached his bed and checked the blankets to see the little green alien snoring happily. Daniel smiled wide as he hadn't lost his new friend. Now, he was back to discovering other planets and their beautiful secrets. Maybe he and the green alien could plant flags together so that people would know he wasn't alone. Either way, this was only one stop on the many adventures he was ready to continue.

Don't judge a book by its cover. Some people can look different from you. They can maybe even sound different from you. But no matter where they're from, they are no stranger to friendship. Treat everyone with kindness and don't be afraid to build friendships from around the world.

The Dream of Sweets

Have you ever felt judged for your passion? Maybe there was a dream you had that not many first agreed with or made fun of. Well, Luca had a passion that didn't seem acceptable to some. But what was that passion? The answer was baking.

Luca had dreams that may appear different to some. He really loved making the best sweets and even dreamed of opening his own shop one day. He could show those around him that he could make something truly amazing and change how sweets were made. He wanted something that would make everyone say, "Wow! This is like nothing I have never tasted before!"

His brother, Alberto, was always supportive of his dream. Of course, that was because he tested all of the sweets his brother made. He also loved sports and was even the star of his baseball team. He loved to get dirty and had a passion for cars. But he would drop all of that in an instant if it meant he could have even a single dessert Luca had made.

Luca made many desserts from sprinkled cupcakes, powdered donuts, and even banana chocolate chip cookies. His baking teacher was very happy with his progress as he was baking almost everyday.

One day, Luca went to Alberto's baseball practice to give him a care package of sweet bread. While he waited for him to finish, some of Alberto's teammates saw him and asked what was in the package. Luca answered them happily that it was sweet bread, and was filled with pride when he told them he made it himself. When the players laughed at him, he frowned as they were mocking his passion.

Luca decided not to wait for Alberto after his practice and went home. When he got home he placed Alberto's package in his bedroom and then went to his own room. He then shut the door, took out a notebook and began to write for hours. Sometimes his writings made him happy and then sometimes they made him frustrated. He would tear out pieces of paper or even scratch out what he wrote at times. He was so focused that he didn't notice Alberto knocking on the door.

"Hey, what are you working on?" asked Alberto.

"I'm working on a special project. Can you ask the coach if I can sell some of my goods at your game this weekend?" asked Luca.

"Yeah, sure..." Alberto nodded. He noticed his brother was very deep in thought and was a little concerned. "I noticed you weren't waiting for me at practice today."

"Yeah, some of your teammates laughed at me for making you sweets, so I thought I'd just leave it on your bed," said Luca. He kept his eyes on his work as he spoke.

"Okay, well I'll definitely talk to them about it."

"No need. I have a plan for this Saturday that will change their minds." Luca smiled.

"Then I'll let you get to it, I guess." Alberto nodded and shut the door, and Luca continued writing into the evening.

The next day, he stayed back in his baking class, mixing all sorts of ingredients together. Sugar, strawberry, bananas, anything he could get his hands on was used to make an assortment of desserts. After mixing different  batches of chocolate and fruit, he believed he was now satisfied with what he had created. Which was a good thing as

 he was covered from head to toe in flour and batter by the time he had finished.

The weekend came and Alberto had a big game. He was doing very well, hitting home runs and catching in the outfield. While he played his best, Luca ran a small baking stand approved by the school. When the game ended, Luca came over to give his brother

some cookies he had saved from the stand. The boys saw him with the bag of sweets and snickered. Alberto gave him a look before happily taking them.

"Joke's on you. I get to eat a delicious treat while you guys sit there and watch," he answered as he munched.

Some of the boys scoffed at him while others secretly wanted to try the cookies. Overall, most of the boys continued to tease Luca and the coach took notice. He came over and asked why the boys were all laughing at Luca. The players explained that Luca was doing something silly instead of doing something like playing sports.

The coach frowned at his team and shook his head. "Don't laugh at Luca. Thanks to his bake stand the team is able to afford new uniforms and gear for each player." He gave Luca a hard pat on the back. The boys couldn't hide the look of shock on their faces. Luca really was a talented baker!

Alberto laughed as he continued to eat his cookies. "That's my brother! Always making the best stuff!"

Luca grinned wide as the players quietly thanked him for his work.

"Would you like to try some of the things I made?" asked Luca, giving a sly grin.

Some of the players were hesitant until the pitcher raised a hand. "I'll try some. I mean, how good could they be?" he shrugged.

Luca went to his stand and pulled out the special batch of cookies he had made for the team. He offered the first one to the pitcher who carefully took a bite.

"Oh my gosh! These are amazing!" he shouted. The team all took a cookie and made noises of joy as the cookies they ate were so delicious. The boys finished their cookies instantly and wanted more. Luca said that was his last batch and the team groaned as they wanted more.

You see, when the baseball players laughed at Luca for making sweets, he wasn't upset that they had made fun of him. No, Luca instead took it as a challenge. His dream was to make the best, if not the most original desserts that no one could laugh at or deny. And now that he had proven that to the team, he was consistently bringing them sweets to every practice and they never laughed at his creations again.

But though he made more desserts for others, he always made sure to give Alberto his best batches. Because above all of the players, his brother was the one who always believed in him the most and supported his dream.

Be yourself, young dreamer. Do what you want to do because it makes you happy. People may laugh and tease you, but you have a dream. Not everyone will support your passion, but that's okay. You want to do something amazing and whether you're a boy who loves sports or a boy who loves to bake, that is your passion. Don't let them take that away.

The Little Navigator

You may have had dreams in the stars, but what about the sea? Have you ever dreamed that you could map out the waters and find your way through the waves? That's a challenge Oliver would have to face. Finding his way back home.

Little Oliver was a pirate who had a dream of mapping the entire sea. He wanted to be the ship's lead navigator one day so that he could get his ship mates out of any danger they may face. But until then, he learned everything he could from the ship's current navigator, Edwardo.

Oliver took as many notes as he could, ranging from the strength of the winds to the movement of the waves. Whenever the pirates stopped on an island, he would spend his allowance on books so he could study the island and everything it had to offer. Whether it was fruit, animals, or even the weather, Oliver wanted to be as prepared as possible in case he ever ended up alone. When he wasn't studying, he would sit with Edwardo and draw maps of the places they had been so that if they ever returned, they knew exactly where to go. Oliver would try very hard in all of that he did so that he could reach his dream, and soon, there would be a day that would test all he had learned.

One day, enemy pirates attacked the ship. They blasted their cannons and came aboard to steal whatever they could. Oliver fought a few pirates himself while Edwardo tried to navigate the ship from the ship's lookout. But when the ship took too many cannons, it began to sink and Oliver's crew had to escape!

Many of Oliver's crew agreed to meet at Parrot Cove as it was the closest island to them. Oliver had collected a few things and tried to go with them, but someone had stopped him! He tried to escape a large scary pirate, but he was too strong and took Oliver back to their ship. Oh no! Oliver had been captured by the enemy pirates! As the captors sailed in the opposite direction, Oliver began to panic.

"I have to get off this ship, fast!" he said. He pulled out a small wire from his pocket and carefully picked the lock of his cell. He heard a clicking sound and the cell opened slowly. He then crept out of the brig and onto the deck where some of the enemy pirates were celebrating their victory. Many watched the sea while others rested on the deck below. Oliver checked the wind with his finger and noticed it was blowing a little harder than normal. To Oliver, that meant the waves would become uneasy very soon. He snuck around to the back of the ship where the row boats were and waited for the wind to pick up even more. As it did, the waves began to rock the ship harder and harder. Because of this, they made a large crashing sound that Oliver used to his advantage. He snuck onto a rowboat and when the waves rocked the ship again, he released the ropes and dropped the boat into the ocean.

With the stolen rowboat, he sailed it through the sea. He was glad he got away safely, but the hard part had begun. He took a deep breath as he tried to remember the lessons Edwardo had taught him.

He held up a finger to check for the wind and then took out a compass out of his pocket. Parrot Cove would be North East. Oliver was nervous but began to row in the direction he thought was correct. So he rowed and rowed for hours until he was tired. He had swiped a canteen of water and snacks from his ship before it sank so that he wouldn't starve. When he finished resting, he continued rowing until he reached an island off in the distance.

"Oh, thank goodness! I made it!" he cheered. He walked onto the island and quickly noticed that none of his crew-mates were there. In fact, no one was there. The island was empty! There were only trees of fruit and sand all around him. "Oh no! I can't believe I came to the wrong island," he cried. How could he direct a ship if he couldn't find the right island? Worse than that, what if he never found Edwardo and his crew? Oliver went to one of the shaded fruit trees and sat down, pulling his knees to his chest.

He kept his head down as all of these thoughts made him very sad. Would he ever find his crew again? Would they even take him back if they knew he was lost? The more he thought about these things, the more sadness he began to feel. What if Edwardo was disappointed in him that he couldn't find his way? Did he not pay attention to what he was taught? He was sure he took his notes very well. Maybe he missed something. He even made sure to read so many books about the different places he had visited. But maybe that was pointless too.

He made a heavy sigh and watched as the waves grew calmer over time. Maybe he should just stay on the island. He didn't want to, but he wasn't sure where to go. The wind picked up again and he began to fall asleep. He didn't realize how tired he was and the island was somewhat relaxing.

As he slept, the wind blew so hard that a fruit fell from a tree and landed next to him, making him jump. He yawned and picked up the fruit and his eyes widened. He recognized this fruit as a mango, something that only grew just a few miles away from Parrot Cove. Maybe he could still find his way back! If that was the case, there was no time to lose!

Oliver stood up and took the mango with him. He pulled out his compass and checked the wind again, realizing he had made a few too many turns. He rowed back through the sea and went left of the island. After rowing for an hour, he saw another island. This time, it held a sign that read Parrot Cove in big wooden letters over the dock. Oliver did it! He'd found the island! He pulled his boat ashore and waved to Edwardo, who ran and gave him a big hug.

"Oliver! I was so worried. How did you find your way here?" asked Edwardo.

"Let's just say you taught me well." Oliver smiled, giving him the mango he had taken from the island before. The two laughed together and the crew celebrated Oliver's return. Some of the crew had even agreed to let him lead their new ship on a few adventures as they were impressed with his skills. He had found his way back to them and truly believed he would make a great navigator one day.

There may be times when you are challenged to use what you have learned. You may make mistakes along the way, even when you're confident. But don't give up. Remember to grow your knowledge of the things around you and don't forget what you've learned.

The Scared Knight

Being brave is a great thing to be when you are chasing your dreams, young dreamer. But that doesn't mean it is always easy. You may find yourself running away, or not sure what to do. But you're not alone in doing so, as William was known well in the kingdom for being a scared knight. But that wouldn't stop him from trying to prove that he too could be brave.

William was a knight who wanted to be brave, and today he would have the chance to do so. The king had announced a challenge that whoever brought back a scale from the fearsome dragon in the valley would be known as the bravest knight in the kingdom. William was excited, but also nervous. The dragon was said to be a very large beast who breathed fire and could blow you away with its large wings.

Not only was the dragon scary, but the journey to its cave was also scary. To reach the dragon, he would have to pass through the forest of trolls.

William waited nervously with the others, and some of the other knights noticed he was competing and laughed at him.

"Didn't Will run away from a pig once?" one of the knights snickered.

"I remember when he was scared of his horse," another knight whispered.

William took a deep breath and waited for the king to announce the start of the competition. When His Majesty blew the trumpet horn, William got on his horse and rode into the distance as the challenge had begun. The first was the forest of trolls. William had his horse trot quietly between the trees. He heard a crunch to his left and looked over to see a troll eating cooked chicken. He was a big and ugly creature with large ears and teeth. He also had large feet as well!

William kept trotting along, keeping his eyes on the troll as they passed, until a troll stepped right in front of him! The horse quickly backed away as William shouted in fear.

"What is a small knight like you doing in our forest?" The troll laughed. William tried to speak, but he was too scared to find the words. The troll laughed more and stepped closer.

"If you can't speak then you should run away before we eat you!" he shouted. He then began to charge at William who was frozen in fear. It wasn't until the troll was just close enough that he pulled the reins back on his horse and began to gallop away from the troll. As he was being chased he looked around for anything that could help him fight off the troll. He had a sword but he was too scared to get off his horse to fight him. He then came up with a plan and directed his horse through the trees. The troll chased him without thought and William began to charge towards a large tree. Right before his horse hit the tree he pulled the horse to go right, to miss hitting it. The troll didn't pay attention and ended up running right into the tree, knocking him out.

William breathed a heavy sigh of relief and quickly made his way out of the forest, being very thankful that he only had to fight the one troll.

Once he'd made it past the forest, he reached the dragon's cave and grew more anxious. He wanted to enter, but his feet were heavy as stones as he thought he could hear the dragon breathe from inside. He clenched his fist and began to feel down.

"Can't do this," he said quietly. He sat by the cave and tried to calm his heart. "I'm not brave enough. What if I get eaten? Or catch on fire if he uses his dragon breath?" He readied his horse to leave when he paused, maybe he was over-thinking it. He had already made it this far and in his heart he didn't want to turn back now. He swallowed his fears and turned back towards the cave. He began to walk forward and entered the cave as his horse waited patiently.

Deep into the cave he went until he reached the dragon's den. He paused when he saw the dragon, who was huge! He was very long from head to tail and had a very big belly. His wings were so large, they covered his body like a blanket. He was also sleeping on a large pile of gold coins!

William exhaled and tiptoed around the beast. He wanted to take a small scale from the dragon's tail, but it was also resting on the gold coins so he would have to climb them in order to reach it. He began to climb but the coins slid down around him making a rattling noise. His heart skipped a beat as he watched the beast's ears move. He stayed very still for a moment until an idea came to mind. He began to put a few gold coins in his pocket and continued to climb. When he reached the tail, he took out his sword and gripped a scale the size of his hand. Just as he was about to cut it, the dragon's tail moved! William felt himself falling and held on tight to the scale! But then the scale came off and he hit the ground with a hard thud!

The dragon awoke and was angry! He turned around just as William had hidden behind a large rock. As it moved, it stomped around and roared! William peeked out from the rock and took one of the gold coins out. He flipped the coin away from him and the dragon ran towards the sound. As he did, William slipped out from the rock and crept closer towards the cave's exit. He then hid again as he thought the dragon had found him. Just like before, he hid and threw a coin away from him to distract the beast. When the time was right, he ran out of the cave and got back on his horse, instructing it to gallop as fast as it could.

He eventually made it back to the kingdom unscathed and trotted past other knights who had failed in their mission to get a dragon's scale. In front of everyone he bowed and presented his trophy to the king who was greatly impressed.

"How did you do it? Did you slay the trolls or fight the dragon?" asked the king.

"No, Your Majesty. I thought quickly and was brave in my own way." William smiled proudly.

"Then, as promised, you will be known as the kingdom's bravest knight!" the king announced. The crowd cheered as William had achieved his dream!

Understand, young dreamer, that you too can be brave. Especially in your own way! You may get scared along the way and that's okay. But you can face any challenge with courage and a little willpower!

The Small Superhero

Have you ever wanted to be a superhero? Maybe you wanted to fly high in the sky or have super strength. You could lift things as heavy as cars, or easily save cats from trees! But what happens when you lose those powers? Well, Matteo would soon find out when he faced off against his biggest villain, the Eraser Man!

Matteo had super powers and always tried to protect his city, Suntropica! He would fly around to look for any citizens in danger and swoop down to save them. Whether it was a bank robbery or someone trying to blow up the city, Matteo was there to save the day! One day, he was fighting his biggest villain, Eraser Man, when he was trapped in a machine. He tried to fight his way out of a large glass bubble that seemed to be unbreakable. Meanwhile, Eraser Man stood by a lever, laughing maniacally.

"Haha! I got you, and now that I do, prepare to have your powers erased!" Eraser Man laughed. He pulled the lever and a bright light shot at Matteo. When the light went away, Matteo was confused.

He didn't feel any different. Even Eraser Man was confused.

Matteo punched the glass bubble with all of his might and broke through. He grabbed Eraser Man and flew him over to the police.

"But I don't understand. My machine was supposed to work!" Eraser Man shouted. He was soon arrested by the police and Matteo flew home. As he did, he began to feel as though he was getting lower to the ground. He tried to fly higher up, but he was only going down! When he landed, he jumped up to fly again, but nothing happened.

"Oh no! My powers are not working!" said Matteo. Not sure what to do, he went to the professor who always made him new suits and gadgets and asked why his powers were not working. After some testing, the professor shrugged.

"It seems that the ray he hit you with has taken your powers away," said the professor.

"Can you bring them back, professor?" Matteo asked worriedly.

"Unfortunately, there's nothing I can do. The good news is that I think they will come back within twenty-four hours. So until then, I would just take it easy."

"Twenty-four hours?! I can't go without my powers for that long. The city needs me!"

"Well, maybe you can help the city in other ways. Until then, there's nothing I can do." The professor shrugged.

Matteo thanked him for his time and left his lab feeling sad. How could Matteo help the city if he didn't have his powers? He couldn't stop trains in emergencies or save people from burning buildings. So what could he do?

Matteo walked down the street and noticed an old woman standing by the light. She looked a little worried and Matteo asked what was wrong.

"Oh, I can't see the lights very well and I need to cross the street. Would you be willing to help me, young man?" asked the old woman. Matteo agreed and took her hand. When the light turned green, Matteo helped her cross the street safely and the old woman was very grateful.

"Thank you so much! Now I can easily get home," she said. She waved goodbye to Matteo and he felt really happy for helping her. He then continued walking home when he saw a woman asking people for help. Matteo asked what was wrong, and the woman looked defeated.

"We really need some volunteers for different projects today." Her shoulders slumped.

"Maybe I can help." Matteo smiled. The woman was overjoyed and gave him his first assignment. First he was to go to the animal shelter. When he got there the workers really needed help giving the dogs bath so they could look great for adoption. Matteo washed the dogs the best he could one by one and some dogs even got adopted that day!

He then got his next assignment, this time was to help serve food at a home-less shelter. He put on a hairnet and be-gan handing out food to the homeless people. After some time passed by, the workers were happy to announce they had served over one hundred people!

Matteo's last assignment was helping many others clean up trash from the streets and highways so that they could help the environment as well as make their streets look nicer. Matteo put on a vest and began to stick cans and plastic into trash bags and helped throw away the trash when their work was done. The highways had never looked so clean before! At the end of the day, Matteo was very tired but was happy that he had done his best. The woman thanked him gratefully and said that none of this could have been accomplished without his help!

Matteo finally made it home and noticed his neighbor was struggling to get groceries in. Though he was tired, he still offered to help his neighbor and carried the bags of groceries up a flight of stairs. His neighbor thanked him for his kindness and gave Matteo an apple for his gratitude.

Once he finished, he went inside his own home, took a bath and then helped his mother with dinner.

"You look like you had a big day." His mother patted his head.

"I did, I volunteered so much today and it was a lot of fun!" said Matteo.

When he finished eating, he went to bed. As he laid there he thought of something. He couldn't help with the big emergencies, but overall, he felt he had done a very super thing today. He'd helped so many people and animals that it didn't feel pointless. He almost forgot that he had even had superpowers for a moment.

He fell asleep and woke up the next day, wondering if his powers had returned. He went outside and to the back of his home and jumped up. He began to soaring through the air and shouted with joy as his powers had returned! But even though his powers had returned, Matteo still continued to volunteer and help with many projects, as he had found more than one way to be super.

Understand, little dreamer, that you can be helpful in many ways. You don't need super strength or the power to fly to know that you make a difference. You can volunteer at your local shelter or even help your neighbors and family around you. You too are super!

A Place on the Field

Have you ever wanted something so much, but you were given something else? You maybe wanted a new toy, but instead you got a different toy that you didn't expect. Giulio would know this very well when he was given an opportunity he did not expect.

Giulio had a dream of being a professional soccer player. Not only did he want to just play soccer, he wanted the position of goalie. He wanted to stop the enemy team from scoring and catch any balls that flew his way! He was very excited when the day for tryouts finally came.

He stopped so many soccer balls from entering the goal! He just knew that because of this, his coach would definitely give him the position he wanted. But as tryouts went on, Giulio found it odd that the coach wanted him to play other spots as well, including being a defender, one who stopped players from getting to the goalie.

When the day ended, he waited patiently with the other players as his coach called out who made the team. When he called Giulio's name, he was so excited! He did it! Now he could play soccer, but wait... he wasn't chosen for goalie.

He was shocked as he thought he did so well. He decided to ask the coach why he didn't get it and the coach simply responded, "I thought you were great as a goalie, but you played even better as a defender."

Giulio was disappointed and went home to sulk. He didn't want the position he got, and wondered if he should just quit. His mother greeted him with a snack and noticed something was wrong.

"What's wrong, Giulio?" she asked with a look of concern.

"I made the team but I didn't make goalie. I don't know, maybe I should quit," Giulio sighed.

"Don't quit just because you didn't get the position you wanted. I want you to go to each game and play your heart out. You never know, you might even love this different position." His mother smiled, shaking her head.

Giulio nodded, but he still felt down. But he worked so hard to be on the team, and he didn't really want to give up on that now. He played his mother's words over in his head and a thought came to mind. Maybe if he played his position really well, the coach would let him be a goalie in the future. The plan had to work! And so, Giulio went to work.

Whenever he was at practice, he listened to everything the coach said. When players came his way he was light on his feet, keeping the ball from getting anywhere near the goal. The more he defended, the more he was beginning to enjoy where he was. He loved to work with his team-mates and even got a lot of compliments from them for his work.

There were some moments where he would participate in being offensive. He would run down the field with his teammates on each side, passing the ball between them and dodging the enemy players. When he had a chance, he would get the ball and score! He loved these plays, but it was something new that he had to learn. He wasn't used to dribbling the ball as he had only planned to be catching it at the goal. But if he wanted to prove himself a good player, he had to put in the work.

Practice didn't always go well, sometimes he would get frustrated. Sometimes he would miss the ball and sometimes he would trip on the ball as well! But no dream is earned without hard work.

Whenever Giulio fell, he would pick himself back up and run again. Whenever an enemy teammate got past him, he would back up and challenge them again. And all of that work was paying off when he played.

Not only was he getting better with each game, but he was also feeling more excited when he played them as well. His heart was racing as he braced the incoming attacks and shook it off whenever a player got by him. One day, the goalie was sick so the coach let him step in. It was Giulio's time to shine! He had finally got to play his dream position in a real game. Everything that he had worked hard for was worth it!

Giulio stepped in the goal and prepared himself for whatever came his way. As the game played throughout the day, Giulio felt something he didn't expect. He didn't feel happy. He stayed alert whenever he saw the ball, but he felt almost... bored. Maybe he was expecting to do more, but as he watched the defenders run around, he began to miss what he did before.

The game ended, and Giulio's team won! Everyone was ready to celebrate, but Giulio felt differently. The coach stopped him before he went home with what sounded like good news.

"Giulio! You did so well today! Maybe you can be our goalie every other game. What do you say?" he asked.

Guilio was silent for a moment before he shook his head. "Actually, coach, I don't think I want to play goalie anymore. I feel like I didn't enjoy it as much. Defender is where I belong and where I think I have the most fun."

The coach was surprised, but then he smiled. "Then you got it!"

He then went to his mother who hugged him tight. "Giulio! I'm so proud of you! You finally got to be a goalie!"

"Yeah, but I think you were right. I actually enjoyed being a defender more and even asked the coach if I could stay in that position as well." Giulio grinned.

"See? That is why you should always take every opportunity seriously. Because what you get might be even better than what you thought you wanted," she said.

So Giulio continued to play as defender and even agreed to play other positions all over the field, realizing he loved to run and score with the ball as well. He still practiced as a goalie in case his team ever needed a back up. But in the end, Giulio was getting closer to his dream, and would go on to be his team's best defender.

You see, young dreamer, sometimes your dreams may change and that's okay! It's why you should treat every opportunity you get with care, as you may find something you truly enjoy.

Nervous Together

Did you ever have a dream of performing for many on a stage, but you were really nervous to do so? Maybe you wanted to show your talent to a big audience but stage fright overcomes you. Well,

Thomas would have to conquer this if he wanted to be a famous musician.

Thomas loved to play the drums. He was always making a rhythmic beat, whether it was with pens and pencils, or with a light tapping of his foot. He loved making beats so much that his parents got him a drum kit for his birthday. He would then play it every day and soon realize he wanted to be one of the greatest drummers in the world!

One day while he was in school, it was announced that there would be a talent show.

"This is great! I can show off my skills!" he said. He went home excited that day and began to practice as much as he could. In fact, he would practice every day until the talent show arrived. Thomas walked on stage, ready to play what he practiced, but there was a problem. When he sat at his drums and looked at the crowd, his heart raced with fear. The crowd waited on him, but before they knew it, Thomas ran off the stage! The teacher asked him if he still wanted to perform, but Thomas shook his head. He went home feeling embarrassed that he had run from the stage. How could be an amazing musician if he couldn't do a talent show?

When he got home he didn't touch his drum set, and instead went straight to bed. When the next day came, Thomas kept his head low as he still felt bad for running away. As he walked through the halls, two boys stopped him in the hallway. He waited for them to make fun of him, but instead, they asked him a question.

"Hey, you play the drums, right?" the first boy asked.

Thomas was surprised for a moment before he nodded his head.

"That's great! My name is Ricardo and this is Antonio. We're looking for a drummer so we can start a band. Would you like to join us?" asked Ricardo.

"We would have to watch you play before you join," Antonio chuckled.

Thomas thought for a moment. "You don't care that I ran off the stage?" he asked.

"Not really. It was probably just first time scares." Antonio shrugged. Thomas smiled as he felt relieved.

After school, the boys went to Thomas's house and he sat at his drum set. Unlike the stage fright he felt before, he picked up his sticks and began to beat hard on the drums. He let the rhythm flow through him and even felt himself having fun! When he finished, Ricardo and Antonio looked at him with shock.

"That was amazing!" Antonio shouted.

"With your skills, we could win the band competition that's coming up in two months!" Ricardo grinned. Thomas was excited, and together the boys spent two months practicing for the competition.

It was a rocky start when they first started playing. But that was because they had to learn how to play together. Ricardo was a guitar player who had a little trouble playing with Thomas because he had never played with a drummer before. After two weeks, they were beginning to mix well and could even make a tune with a random beat. Then there was Antonio who wrote lyrics while the two played together. Once they were finished, the band slowly came together and blended their talents well. The more they practiced the more confident Ricardo and Antonio were feeling towards the competition. Thomas, on the other hand, grew more and more nervous as time went on. Ricardo noticed this and always stayed a little late after practice to give him a pep talk.

"You can easily do this. You have a lot of skill, and we're going to rock the competition!" said Ricardo. Thomas would nod and even smile a little bit. But deep down he could feel himself shaking.

When it was the night of the competition, Thomas peeked out to see how big the crowd would be. To his surprise there were many more people there than at the talent show! Ricardo put a hand on his shoulder, making him jump.

"You okay?" He asked.

"I'm way too nervous. What if we don't do well?" said Thomas.

"Don't think about that. Just think about the awesome music we'll make." Ricardo smiled.

A man went on stage and announced Thomas's band and the boys walked on and got into their positions. Thomas waited for his cue but when he looked up, Ricardo and Antonio...were frozen. They too were nervous.

Thomas was surprised...and even relieved. He wasn't the only one who was scared in front of a crowd! Thomas smiled. He wasn't alone, and then he did something he didn't think he could do. He raised his hands, tapped his sticks together and began to play a beat. With the tap of the drums Antonio and Ricardo broke out of their trance. They looked back at Thomas playing with a smile on his face and followed suit, grinning as they joined in! The crowd cheered as they performed and at the end of the competition, the band even got second place!

"I can't believe we did it!" said Ricardo.

"Yeah, and it was all thanks to Thomas. You're a lot braver than I thought!" Antonio gave Thomas a pat on the back.

"Thanks, but you guys actually made me feel better. I was worried I was the only one who would be nervous, but because you were nervous with me, I guess it made me feel okay." Thomas shrugged.

"Well, we definitely understand why you ran off the stage, that crowd can be terrifying." Ricardo nodded.

The boys took home their second place trophy and vowed to do even better next time. The band practiced a few days a week, but Thomas would practice the drums every day so that he could be the best drummer in the world. The band would still go on to play other competitions and even the talent show. And though Thomas would still get very nervous, he would always be the one to break that spell of anxiety.

Remember, young dreamer, that you are not the only one who may get nervous from time to time. Sometimes even the most confident people around you will feel just as scared as you, so shake off your fears and play your heart out!

The Boy and His Horse

Did you ever have to choose between something you wanted to and something you needed to do? Maybe you wanted to participate in a big event but something came up. Well, a little cowboy named Samuel would face this dilemma as he and his horse go to town to compete.

Samuel grew up on a ranch and learned to take care of many different kinds of animals. He liked feeding small chicks, petting goats, and herding cattle. But if there was one animal he loved the most, it was horses. Not only did he love them, but he loved to ride fast on them. Samuel's dream was to be a professional barrel racer. For those who don't know what barrel racing is, it's when you race your horse around an area with barrels and you can't knock the barrel down or it's a penalty!

Samuel already had some experience with barrel racing as his home town always hosted a rodeo once every year. During the rodeo, kids his age could barrel race for a first place ribbon. Samuel collected those ribbons every year for three years straight and it was all thanks to his trusty horse, Hollow.

Samuel loved Hollow with all of his heart and made sure to take very good care of him. Any time he visited him, he made sure to clean him, take care of his feet and give him lots of pets. When his family wasn't looking, he would sneak him extra treats and Hol-low would neigh gratefully. When they were out in the pen, Samuel set up the barrels and would practice for the best recorded time and Hollow would do his best to avoid them. They made a great team together and Sam was ready to prove that for the fourth year in a row to his town! Practices were going so well that he knew they could win!

On the day of the competition, Samuel loaded his horse into the trailer and noticed that Hollow wasn't walking like normal.

"What's the matter, boy? Are you okay?" asked Samuel. Hollow gave a low neigh and he became concerned. He tried to look for any scratches on his legs but didn't see any so far.

"It's okay, boy, we're gonna rock the competition today! I can't wait to pin another ribbon on top of your stall!" He grinned. Hollow gave a more excited whinney and the two headed into town where they were greeted by the locals. As he unloaded his horse, his best friend Gabriel went over to him.

"Hey, Sam, I see Hollow is looking good as ever," said Gabriel.

"Thanks, I'm a little worried about him today. He seems to be walking a little slow."

"I'm sure he's just a little nervous. You get out there and win those ribbons, okay?" Gabriel waved. Samuel tipped his cowboy hat to his friend and began prepping for the race. Though he was known to do the barrel race, Samuel also participated in other rodeo events such as using his horse to rope a cow and junior bull riding, which he never really did that well at.

The first was bull riding. As said before, Samuel wasn't that great at bull riding, as the bull would buck him off at every opportunity. He never lasted long but he always joined in because it made him feel like a real cowboy! As soon as he got thrown off, he got up, dusted himself off and then cheered for Gabriel as his friend took first place every year! After the event was over, he saddled up Hollow and got ready for the cattle roping. The goal was to throw a rope around a cow while he rode fast on his horse. The event began and Samuel gave a verbal signal to Hollow.

"Gallop! Gallop!" Samuel shouted. Hollow began to run faster and faster and Samuel directed him carefully. He raised his rope to throw at the cattle when he began to feel wobbly. Before he knew it, Hollow had collapsed! Samuel hit the ground hard and the crowd shouted around him. His family ran into the arena and picked him up. He was a little dizzy as his father sat him up and his mother gave him a bag of ice to put on his head.

"Sweetheart, are you okay?" his mother asked.

"Where's Hollow?" Samuel looked around. He tried to look past his parents and noticed his horse was being carted off towards the vet tent. His eyes widened and he ran towards the tent. When he went in, he saw the local vet checking on Hollow's leg.

"Doctor, is he okay?" Samuel asked in a panic.

The vet wrapped Hollow's leg and gave a reassuring smile. "He'll be alright, he just has a light sprain. You two are lucky that it wasn't worse. Either way, he just needs some time to heal."

Samuel was relieved and hugged his horse who happily nudged him. Gabriel ran into the tent and pointed outside.

"Sam! The barrel race is starting. Aren't you going to compete?" he asked.

"I can't really compete if my horse is hurting." Samuel scratched his head.

"Yeah, my dad and I saw what happened. We are willing to loan you our horse so you can still race. You can still win your ribbon this year!" Gabriel grinned. Samuel was shocked and thought about leaving for a moment. He could still get that ribbon and continue building on his dream. But when he looked back at Hollow, he knew in his heart that the victory wouldn't be the same without him.

"I think I'll have to pass this year. There's always next year and besides, it just wouldn't feel right without the horse who always helps me win." Sam looked back at Hollow. Gabriel nodded and Samuel went back to talking to the vet on how to take care of Hollow's ankle.

When the day ended, all he could think about was making sure his horse was okay. His father came up to him while he was shoveling hay and smiled at him.

"I'm proud of you, son," he said.

"Why? I didn't win anything this year." Samuel looked at him confused.

"No, but you chose to take care of the one you love and it takes a big heart to do that."

Samuel grinned as he looked at Hollow. "Thanks, Dad."

Remember, young dreamer, take care of the ones you love. Whether it's your parents, or your pet. Treasure your time with them as they'll be with you as you grow.

The Wizard and the Singer

Is there a subject you would love to study, but it seems a little hard to learn? Maybe you want to study space, or the ocean, but you struggle to understand the material. What about the subject of magic? That's where our hero, Nicholas, comes into the picture.

Nicholas wanted to be a powerful wizard who went on quests with his friends. Only, Nicholas was not a great wizard... and he didn't have any friends. He did practice his magic every day, but it always came with...unexpected results.

He would stand in his yard with a spell book in one hand and the other hand would be raised. He read his book carefully, some would say maybe too carefully, and then aimed at a target he made.

"Alacafire!" he would shout, hoping to conjure a fire. But instead of flames, he conjured a blizzard! He waved his hand in a panic and the blizzard left with him wiping snow off of his robe. He then tried a different spell in his book in hope that it would go right this time. He held up his hand and took a deep breath. "Ala-calightning!" He waited patiently but instead of lightning, there was only rain. He waved his hand again and the rain disappeared.

Irritated, he continued to look through his book. It was very important that wizards stuck closely to the book as that was how he was taught. But no matter how much he studied his spells, he just couldn't get it right.

After the last spell ended with conjuring many chickens, Nicholas checked his small watch and noticed the market would be open soon. With a heavy sigh, he tucked his book away in his robe and made his way to the center of the village. It was already very crowded as knights and elves searched for people to help them on their upcoming quests.

Nicholas sat in the wizard corner feeling gloomy. No one ever picked him as they also knew his magic was faulty.

As many wizards began to leave with their groups, Nicholas was ready to give up. That was, until a singer with a guitar called out to him.

"You there! Lone wizard!" The singer gave him a friendly wave. Nicholas was shocked for a moment and even pointed at himself to make sure that he was the one being called.

"Yes, you! You look lonely, and I'd like some company on a quest. Would you like to come with me?" The singer grinned.

"...You've heard I'm not very good with spells, right?" Nicholas couldn't hide his puzzlement.

"I have. But at the end of the day, I need a wizard and it sounds like no one has given you a chance. And besides, all I have is a guitar so I'm never really picked for quests myself. So, what do you say? I've heard it's not too hard of a quest."

Nicholas was almost certain that the singer was crazy. Who went on a quest with just a guitar? But at the same time, he wasn't sure when the next opportunity to travel with another would arise. He reluctantly agreed and the singer strummed a tune in excitement.

"Wonderful! My name is Frederick," said the singer, holding out a hand and smiling.

"And I'm Nicholas." The wizard smiled back, shaking his hand. The two began their journey to a small cave a little ways from the village. When they reached the entrance, there was a heavy boulder in their way.

"Do you think you could move that boulder?" asked Fredrick. Nicholas hesitantly took out his book and looked at a spell. He held his hand out and shut his eyes hoping it would go well.

"Moveth boulderous!" he shouted. The two waited as the boulder didn't move. All of a sudden, other rocks began to fall and an even heavier boulder fell in front of the one they tried to move! Nicholas looked at Fredrick who simply laughed.

"Don't worry, I'm sure there's another way in." He smiled. He began to walk around and Nicholas silently followed, feeling embarrassed. Lucky for them both, there was a small crack in the side where they could slip through. From there, they traveled down a path and

Nicholas took a small torch out of his robe. He tapped the top of the stick and a small flame appeared so that they could see their path. Small magic like making a simple fire with a finger was easy, but the spells used in combat were troublesome.

While they walked, Fredrick began to make conversation. "I bet you go on a lot of these adventures."

"Actually, this is my first one. No one ever picks me for these things," Nicholas answered quietly.

"Really? Why?"

"You saw what happened with the boulder. I'm not good with spells, and no one wants a wizard who can't do magic well. I want to be an amazing wizard one day. But now I'm starting to think I'll never get there." Nicholas sighed.

Frederick saw the sadness in Nicholas's eyes and gave him a nudge. "I think you're a great wizard!"

"Really?" Nicholas eyed him.

"Anyone who studies hard and can even do magic is amazing! I wish I could, but I love the power of song too much. The point is, you should be proud of what you can do. Maybe instead of doing everything by the book, you should do magic in your own way."

"Huh, I never really thought about it that way." Nicholas smiled.

The two continued deeper into the cave until they reached an open area where Fredrick spotted a treasure chest. Unfortunately, it was being guarded by a huge troll who saw them walk in and started to attack!

The two dodged and Fredrick began to play a calming song with his guitar to see if he could calm the beast with music. The troll swung at him and they realized it wasn't working.

"Any ideas?" he called out to Nicholas.

Nicholas quickly flipped through his spell book to see if he could help the singer, but nothing really seemed right.

He then remembered what Fredrick said and put his spell book away.

He was going to make his own spell. He put his hand out towards Fredrick and hesitated. He could see his friend getting tired and soon the troll was walking towards him! Nicholas thought for a moment then he said the spell, only a little different.

"Sound wavis increaseth!" he shouted. Frederick watched his guitar glow and faced towards the monster. He brought his arm up and then forced it down on his guitar creating a heavy sound that shook the whole dungeon! Rocks fell from the roof, crushing the troll and the two cheered as they had defeated the beast!

Nicholas and Fredrick took home the chest where they had found gold inside!

After this, the two would go on many more adventures together and Nicholas would learn to perfect his own spells and realized he loved to do magic that was his.

You see, young dreamer, it can be hard to learn about your passions and it can take a lot of focus. But know that if you truly believe in yourself then you too can make your own achievements.

The Big Wave

Throughout this book you have expe-
rienced many stories about courage,
friendship, and heroism. What do you
think you have learned so far? What was

your favorite story? They all teach wonderful lessons, but there is one more story you must hear. This is the story of Ezio and the giant wave.

Ezio grew up by the sea and learned to surf when he was very young. As he got older he rode the waves with confidence and even rode some that others wouldn't dare try. And one day, he wished to ride the greatest wave in the world.

When he finished surfing, he and his siblings would help his uncle make dinner and they would sit around the campfire. As they did, Ezio would beg him to tell the story of the Wave of Isabelle. His siblings would groan as he laughed. It was a story he had told so many times before, but he always made sure to tell it to Ezio like it was his first time hearing it.

"It was said that long ago in ancient times there was a girl named Isabelle who wanted to sail all over the world, but she couldn't because her family said it was too dangerous. Because of this, she would watch the sea everyday, praying that one day she would be a part of it. The sea held beauty, adventure, and freedom; all of the things she longed for. And then one day, her wish would come true. Her soul would mend with the ocean and every century she was said to return in the biggest wave ever because she missed her home. Anyone who is brave enough to ride the wave will see Isabelle herself and she'll show you the ocean's soul." Ezio's uncle put his hands up in the air.

"Do you believe in the story, Uncle?" asked Ezio.

"I do, Ezio. Many have given up on the wave, but I believe she is coming back."

"I hope so, as it's my dream to surf it one day." Ezio smiled.

As the months passed on, Ezio waited for the wave of Isabelle. He would still surf like normal but deep in his heart, he wished his dream would come true. Then one day, something strange happened.

The sky was clear and the sun shined bright on Ezio as he waited on his surfboard in the ocean. Then, within a few minutes, the skies turned dark, but there were no clouds. In the distance, Ezio could hear what he thought was a low guttural roar.

He looked ahead and saw a wave that rose higher and higher. Ezio's heart raced as he didn't think the wave would stop growing! Was this it? The wave of Isabelle? Ezio wanted to get away. He didn't want to be swallowed!

He began to swim away as fast as he could until he realized, this was the wave he had always wanted. He would never see a wave like this again and it was one that no one had ever surfed before. If he did this, he would achieve his dream.

He looked back at the wave and fear flooded through him as the wave grew closer. No. He had made up his mind. He was going to surf it!

He prepared his stance and before he knew it he was riding up the wave! His legs felt like jelly, but he was determined to stand on his board. As he did, he smiled wide as he was riding the greatest wave man would ever know. As he rode it, he looked into the wave and almost fell off as he saw a girl laughing at him, in the wave! She held out a hand and Ezio instinctively reached for it. He felt himself getting pulled into the water and he shut his eyes tight.

"Don't be scared," a voice echoed.

He opened his eyes and a girl his age giggled at him. He looked around and realized he was floating deep in the sea, but he could breathe like normal.

But what he saw was practically breathtaking. It was the true beauty of the sea. Creatures he had never seen before swam around him and the reefs were colorful and vibrant.

"It's beautiful, isn't it?" asked Isabelle.

"Yeah. Am I dreaming?" Ezio looked at her and she continued to giggle.

"No. It may seem that way, but what you are seeing is the soul of the ocean, something no one else may see in their life." Isabelle grinned. She let him look around a bit longer before she lightly tapped his forehead.

His body began to feel heavy and he thought he could feel his body sinking deeper in the water. He then began to feel sleepy and felt everything go dark. When he opened his eyes, his uncle was holding him in his arms, calling his name in a panic.

"Ezio! Are you okay? Can you hear me?"

Ezio realized he was back on the beach and slumped his shoulders as what he saw was feeling more and more like a dream. "I'm fine, I guess I just fell asleep." He shrugged.

"No, Ezio. You rode the wave of Isabelle! You were as high as the stars and then you disappeared!" his uncle shouted. Ezio's eyes widened. It wasn't a dream! He really did see the ocean's true beauty!

"Tell me, what did you see?" asked his uncle excitedly.

"I saw Isabelle. She was happy and laughing, and when she pulled me in, she showed me the soul of the sea. It was amazing, Uncle!" Ezio grinned.

"That's my boy! Even if you hadn't seen her, you still surfed the greatest wave that no one ever had, and that takes courage."

Ezio nodded his head and looked out to the sea, hoping that one day Isabelle may visit him again.

Remember this, no matter what, young dreamer, no dream is too big to conquer. Even the scariest of moments will be outshined by the courage you put into your goals. Be who you want to be and conquer the fear as you journey to achieve your dreams.

Epilogue

Little Dreamer, you've been on quite the journey.

Did you see how the boys in this book made their dreams come true? Now, think about what *your* dreams are. What is it that you want to do? Everyone's dream may be different, but just like the heros you have read about, you have everything you need inside of you to reach your goals and your passions. Whether your dreams consist of performing on stage the best or navigating the seas, big or small they are yours to achieve. Just like them, you have courage, strength, and unique characteristics that are yours alone. If you have the confidence to believe in how special you are, all of your dreams can become realities.

So tell me, Little Dreamer, what is *your* dream?

Bonuses
Our Gifts For you

Subscribe to our Newsletter and receive these free materials

Scan Me

www.specialartbooks.com/free-materials/

Stay Connected with Us

Instagram: @specialart_coloring
Facebook Group: Special Art – Kids Entertainment
Website: www.specialartbooks.com

Impressum

For questions, feedback, and suggestions:
support@specialartbooks.com

Nadia Ross, Special Art

Copyright © 2021

www.specialartbooks.com

Images by © Shutterstock

Made in United States
North Haven, CT
01 December 2022

27683991R00059